Geronimo Stilton ENGLISH!

27 MOVING AROUND 我喜歡到處去

新雅文化事業有限公司
www.sunya.com.hk

Geronimo Stilton English
MOVING AROUND 我喜歡到處去

作　　者：Geronimo Stilton 謝利連摩・史提頓
譯　　者：申倩
責任編輯：王燕參
封面繪圖：Giuseppe Facciotto
插圖繪畫：Claudio Cernuschi, Andrea Denegri, Daria Cerchi
內文設計：Angela Ficarelli, Raffaella Picozzi
出　　版：新雅文化事業有限公司
香港英皇道499號北角工業大廈18樓
電話：（852）2138 7998
傳真：（852）2597 4003
網址：http://www.sunya.com.hk
電郵：marketing@sunya.com.hk
發　　行：香港聯合書刊物流有限公司
香港新界大埔汀麗路36號中華商務印刷大廈3字樓
電話：（852）2150 2100　傳真：（852）2407 3062
電郵：info@suplogistics.com.hk
印　　刷：C & C Offset Printing Co.,Ltd
香港新界大埔汀麗路36號
版　　次：二〇一二年七月初版
10 9 8 7 6 5 4 3 2 1

Original title: ANDARE IN GIRO
Based upon an original idea by Elisabetta Dami
www.geronimostilton.com

ISBN: 978-962-08-5626-6

18/F, North Point Industrial Building, 499 King's Road, Hong Kong
Published and printed in Hong Kong

CONTENTS
目錄

BENJAMIN'S CLASSMATES
班哲文的老師和同學們

Benjamin
班哲文

Hsing
阿星

Laura
羅拉

Kiku
奇哥

Antonia
安東妮婭

Liza
麗莎

GERONIMO AND HIS FRIENDS

謝利連摩和他的家鼠朋友們

謝利連摩・史提頓 Geronimo Stilton

一個古怪的傢伙，簡直可以說是一隻笨拙的文化鼠。他是《鼠民公報》的總裁，正花盡心思改變報紙業的歷史。

菲・史提頓 Tea Stilton

謝利連摩的妹妹，她是《鼠民公報》的特派記者，同時也是一個運動愛好者。

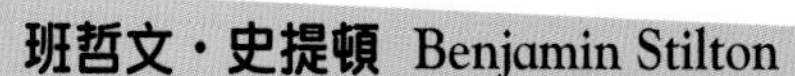

班哲文・史提頓 Benjamin Stilton

謝利連摩的小侄兒，常被叔叔稱作「我的小乳酪」，是一隻感情豐富的小老鼠。

潘朵拉・華之鼠 Pandora Woz

柏蒂・活力鼠的姨甥女、班哲文最好的朋友，是一隻活潑開朗的小老鼠。

柏蒂・活力鼠 Patty Spring

美麗迷人的電視新聞工作者，致力於她熱愛的電視事業。

賴皮 Trappola

謝利連摩的表弟，非常喜歡食物，風趣幽默，是一隻饞嘴、愛開玩笑的老鼠，善於將歡樂傳遞給每一隻鼠。

麗萍姑媽 Zia Lippa

謝利連摩的姑媽，對鼠十分友善，又和藹可親，只想將最好的給身邊的鼠。

艾拿 Iena

謝利連摩的好朋友，充滿活力，熱愛各項運動，他希望能把對運動的熱誠傳給謝利連摩。

史奎克・愛管閒事鼠 Ficcanaso Squitt

謝利連摩的好朋友，是一個非常有頭腦的私家偵探，總是穿着一件黃色的乾濕褸。

HAVING A WALK WITH GERONIMO

與謝利連摩一起散步

親愛的小朋友，今天柏蒂到學校去接班哲文和潘朵拉放學，他們一起騎單車回來。你也想跟班哲文和潘朵拉一樣騎單車在妙鼠城裏逛逛嗎？我以一千塊莫澤雷勒乳酪發誓，在城市的大街小巷內騎單車，或乘坐公共交通工具，或散步是多麼愉快的事啊！今天就讓我帶你們在妙鼠城裏到處逛逛吧！我們還可以一邊逛一邊學習道路標誌和交通規則呢。

Geronimo Stilton
See you later!
Let's park our bicycles here!
Ok, Benjamin!

our 我們的

跟我謝利連摩·史提頓一起學英文，
就像玩遊戲一樣簡單好玩！

你可以一邊看着圖畫一邊讀。
以下有幾個標誌，你要特別留意：

- 當看到 標誌時，你可以聽CD，一邊聽，一邊跟着朗讀，還可以跟着一起唱歌。

- 當看到 標誌時，你可以和朋友們一起玩遊戲，或者嘗試回答問題。題目很簡單，它們對鞏固你所學過的內容很有幫助。

- 當看到 標誌時，你要注意看一下格子裏的生字，反覆唸幾遍，掌握發音。

最後，不要忘記完成小測驗和練習冊裏的問題！看看你有多聰明吧。

祝大家學得開開心心！

謝利連摩·史提頓

ON FOOT 步行

今天天氣晴朗，妙鼠城的交通很順暢。我帶着班哲文和潘朵拉四處走走，並教他們如何過馬路。你也跟着一起學習吧！

Let's cross at the traffic lights!

Before crossing the street at the zebra crossing, let's first look right and then left.

THE TRAFFIC LIGHTS
交通燈

我們在交通燈前停下來。我向班哲文和潘朵拉解釋不同顏色的交通燈代表的意思。

red	Stop!
yellow	Stop and wait!
green	Walk!

✪ 觀察下面兩種情況，圖中的孩子過馬路的方法正確嗎？正確的，就把 Right 圈起來；不正確的，就把 Wrong 圈起來。

A SONG FOR YOU!

Traffic Lights

When I'm walking
down the street,
the traffic lights help me.
And they say to me
oh walk, it's green!

Green means go!
Yellow means watch out!
And red means stop, stop!

When I'm walking down the street,
the traffic lights help me.
And they say to me
oh stop, it's red!

Red means stop!
Yellow means watch out!
And green means go, go!
When the traffic lights are green, go!
When the traffic lights are red, stop!
When the traffic lights are yellow,
stop, stop and watch out!

答案：1.Right 2. Wrong

VEHICLES 車輛
快到交通繁忙時間了，馬路上的車輛開始多起來。班哲文和潘朵拉想知道各種車輛的英文名稱怎麼說，於是我逐一給他們介紹。你也跟着一起學習吧！
Motorcyclists must go slowly!
Everybody must stop when an ambulance goes by!
Car drivers must drive carefully!
car
ambulance
bus
sports car
off-road vehicle
slow 慢
slowly 慢慢地
fast 快
too fast 太快
go by 經過
must 一定

This car driver is
driving slowly: that's ok!
taxi
TAXI
police car
This motorcyclist
is driving too fast:
that's no good!
WRRROOOOOOOOM
motorcycle,
motorbike
fire engine
train
用英語說出以下的詞彙：
汽車、電單車。
答案：car, motorcycle / motorbike

ROAD SIGNS
道路標誌

班哲文想在潘朵拉面前顯示自己已經認識所有道路標誌了，但他不知道這些道路標誌用英語該怎麼說，所以我便向他一一說明。你也跟着一起學習吧！

1

Pedestrian area, no vehicles.

2

Cycle lane for cyclists.

3

Children's crossing: slow down.

4

No parking.

5

Stop!

6

Parking.

7

No noise in this area!

8

No entry.

★ 這三個道路標誌代表什麼意思？用英語說出來。

1. 

2. 

3. 

答案：1. No parking.
2. Stop!
3. Parking.

THE TRAFFIC OFFICER
交通警察

為了讓繁忙的交通保持順暢，一位交通女警趕來指揮交通。潘朵拉想知道交通女警的每個手勢各代表什麼意思，於是我跟她逐一說明。你也跟着一起學習吧。

A

Move along, please!

B

Stop!

C

Stop, you've committed a traffic offence!

D

Go that way!

✪ 下面兩幅圖中，交通警察應該控告哪輛汽車的司機呢？選出正確的答案，在空格內加 ✓。

1

- ☐ Driver 1
- ☐ Driver 2
- ☐ Both drivers

2

答案：Both drivers

I CAN DRIVE 我會開車

我、班哲文和潘朵拉來到石頭廣場，我們約了菲和史奎克．愛管閒事鼠在這裏見面。菲開着一輛紅色的跑車，而史奎克則騎着他的香蕉色電單車。馬路上還有其他汽車和司機，一起跟着我們用英語說說看吧！

Look! Here's Tea in her car!
I can ride a motorcycle.
I can drive a car!
And there's Ficcanaso on his motorcycle!
Ficcanaso is riding his motorcycle.
Tea is driving her car.

I can 我會 / 我能夠
I can't 我不會 / 我不能夠
Can you...? 你會……？ / 你能夠……？

Mummy can drive: she has got a driving licence.

Can you drive a car, Mummy?
Of course! I have a driving licence.

I can't overtake that car!

This motorcyclist pays attention to road signs. Very good!

Can you drive a bus, Dad?
No! I have a driving licence, I can drive a car, but I can't drive a bus!

Dad has got a driving licence, but he can't drive a bus!

THE CYCLE LANE　單車徑

回家的時候，我、班哲文和潘朵拉遇見了騎着單車的艾拿。艾拿停下車子跟我們打招呼，並邀請我們跟他一起騎單車兜風，在妙鼠城有很多單車徑呢！

Let's go for a bicycle ride!

GERONIMO'S HOUSE

Pietra Che Canta Square

Borgonutto Street

Fusillo Street

Scaramazzi Square

Lo Gnocco Avenue

Marinara Square

Sgombro Street

FISH MARKET

Cycling is really tiring!

What a great idea, Iena!

I like riding my bicycle!

street	街道
square	廣場
corner	角落
avenue	大街

turn right 向右轉
turn left 向左轉
cross the street 橫過街道
go through 穿過
go back 回去

Let's go down Borgoratto Street!

Let's stop in Marinara Square!

Let's go down Sgombro Street,
along the seafront!

Let's turn right at the fish market corner!

Let's cross the street at the zebra crossing
in Lo Gnocco Avenue!

Let's go through Scaramazza Square!

Let's go back along Fusillo Street!

Let's go to Pietra Che Canta Square and...

... let's go home!

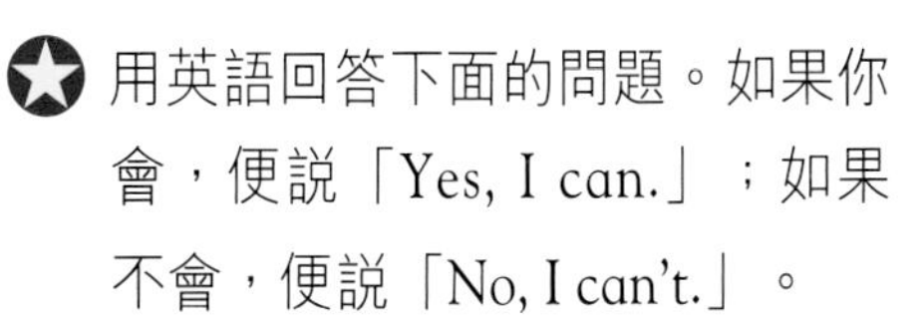

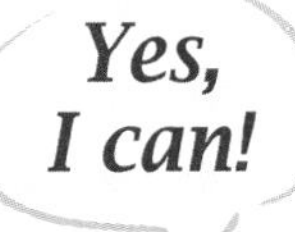

用英語回答下面的問題。如果你會，便說「Yes, I can.」；如果不會，便說「No, I can't.」。

Yes, I can!

No, I can't!

ride a bicycle
騎單車

Can you ride a bicycle?

MY BICYCLE 我的單車

回到家裏，班哲文和潘朵拉想知道單車每個部分的英文名稱怎麼說，於是我便向他們逐一講解。你也跟着一起學習吧！

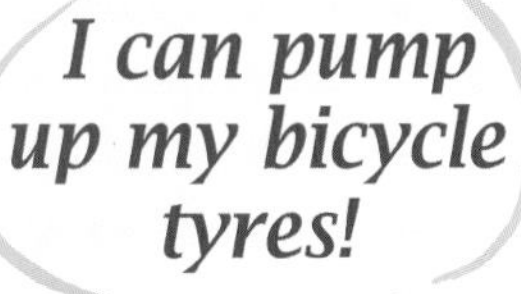

1. 試着用英語說出：「我能夠給我的單車輪胎充氣。」

A SONG FOR YOU!

pump up the tyres
給輪胎充氣
clean
清潔

I Like My Bicycle

I like to ride my bicycle
with my sister or with my brother,
I can ride my bicycle
on a cycle lane or in the park.

It's beautiful to have a bicycle
orange, green or yellow, too.
And travelling around this happy park
and I can ring the bell.

I often clean my bicycle!

I like to ride my bicycle
with my mother or with my father,
I can meet so many friends
and I can play with them.

It's beautiful to have a bicycle
orange, green or yellow, too.
And travelling around this happy park
and I can ring the bell.

It's beautiful to have a bicycle
orange, green or yellow, too.
And travelling around this happy park
and I can ring the bell.

2. 你有單車嗎？它是什麼顏色的？試着用英語說出來。

My bicycle is ...

答案：1. I can pump up my bicycle tyres.

Track 3
A BICYCLE RIDE
The sun is shining: it's a perfect day for some healthy exercise. Iena visits Geronimo in his office and suggests a bicycle ride.
Tea, Benjamin and Pandora are in the office, too. They all decide to go for a bicycle ride together.
I want you fit, fit, fit!
Pity that cycling is tiring!
But bicycles don't pollute the air and the environment!

〈單車之旅〉

今天陽光普照，最適合做一些健康的運動。艾拿到謝利連摩的辦公室來探望他，並提議來一趟單車之旅。

菲、班哲文和潘朵拉也在辦公室裏。他們決定一起去騎單車。

艾拿：我想你的身體一直保持強健，強健，強健！

謝利連摩：可惜騎單車會令人感到很疲累。

菲：但騎單車不會污染空氣和環境。

Iena, Geronimo, Tea, Benjamin, and Pandora get on their bicycles.
Why don't we go to the park?
Yes! Great!
Let's go to the pond to see the swans!

艾拿、謝利連摩、菲、班哲文和潘朵拉各自騎上了他們的單車。

艾拿：我們何不去公園呢？

潘朵拉：對，太好了！

班哲文：我們一起去池塘看天鵝吧！

Pandora suggests a race to see who will get to the pond first.
Shall we race to the pond?
Ok guys, but be careful!

潘朵拉提議大家來一場比賽，看誰最先到達池塘。

潘朵拉：我們來比賽，看誰最先到達池塘，好嗎？

艾拿：好的，但大家要小心！

There are two paths leading to the pond, one is short, the other one is long.

有兩條路通往池塘，其中一條路程較短，另一條路程較長。

Benjamin and Pandora can't wait to go.
Ready? Go!

班哲文和潘朵拉急不及待要出發了。

艾拿：準備好了嗎？出發！

艾拿騎着單車，一直跟在謝利連摩身旁，為他打氣。

艾拿：謝利連摩，加快點吧！
謝利連摩：呼……呼……

但是，不一會兒，便只剩下謝利連摩單獨一個。

謝利連摩：他們在哪裏呢？

謝利連摩看到一個指示牌，他停下來，拿出他的水瓶喝水。

謝利連摩：我想這條路是正確的。

接着，謝利連摩來到一個轉彎處，他感到很疲累，而且滿身是汗。他拐了一個彎，然後……

謝利連摩：他們都在這裏！
謝利連摩按響單車鈴，跟大家打招呼！

菲：看，謝利連摩，你做到了！

謝利連摩：對，但我是最後一個。

潘朵拉嘗試給他一點鼓勵……
潘朵拉：對，但只是因為你選擇了較長的那條路而已。

TEST 小測驗

1. 用英語說出下面的詞彙。

(a) 街道　(b) 行人道　(c) 行人　(d) 斑馬線　(e) 交通燈

2. 讀出下面有關過馬路的英文句子，你知道它們的意思嗎？用中文說說看。

(a) Let's walk on the pavement!
(b) Let's cross at the traffic lights!
(c) Before crossing the street, first look right and then left.

3. 下面的交通燈信號各代表什麼意思？用英語說說看。

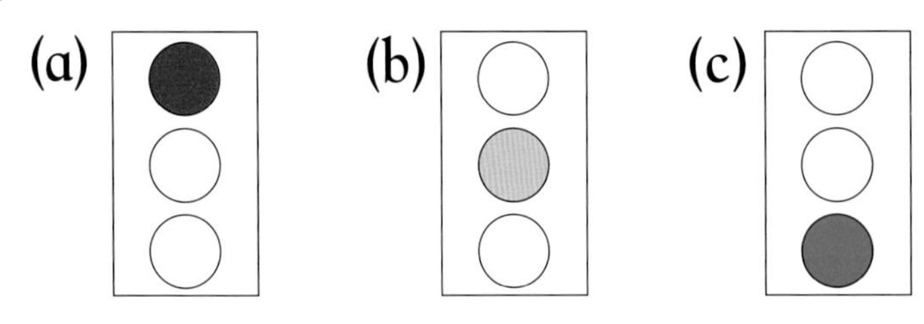

4. 你還記得下面這些車輛用英語該怎麼說嗎？說說看。

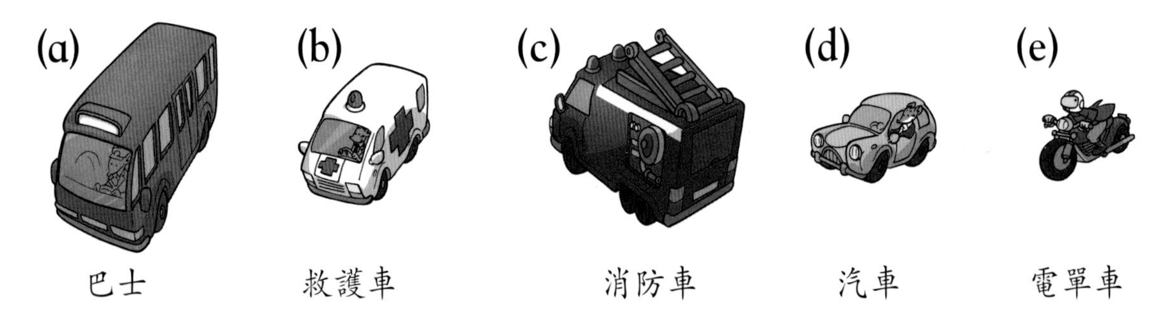

巴士　救護車　消防車　汽車　電單車

5. 下面哪一個句子的意思是「慢點走！」？把代表答案的英文字母圈起來。

A. Go slowly!　B. Stop when an ambulance goes by!

6. 用英語說出下面的句子。

(a) 我會開車。

(b) 我不會開車。

(英、粵、普發聲)

DICTIONARY 詞典

A

air 空氣

alone 單獨

along 沿着

ambulance 救護車

avenue 大街

B

beautiful 美麗

before 之前

bell 鈴

bend 轉彎處

bicycle 單車

brake 剎車掣(普:剎車)

brother 哥哥/弟弟

bus 巴士

C

car 汽車

carefully 小心地

chain 單車鏈

cheer on 打氣

children 孩子

clean 清潔

committed 犯(罪)

corner 角落

cross 橫過

cycle lane 單車徑

D

decide 決定

drive 駕駛

driver 司機

driving licence 駕駛執照

E

entry 進入

environment 環境

exercise 運動

F

fast 快

father 爸爸

fire engine 消防車

first 最先

fish market 魚市場

friends 朋友

front light 車頭燈
（普：車前燈）

G

go back 回去

go through 穿過

green 綠色

H

handlebars （單車）把手

healthy 健康的

here 這裏

I

idea 主意

L

last 最後

left 左

M

meet 遇見

mother 媽媽

motorbike 電單車
（普：摩托車）

motorcycle 電單車
（普：摩托車）

motorcyclist 騎電單車的人
（普：騎摩托車的人）

must 一定

N

noise 噪音

O

office 辦公室

off-road vehicle

越野車

on foot 步行

orange 橙色

overtake 超越

P

park 泊車（普：停車）

pavement 行人道

pedal 踏板

pedestrian 行人

police car 警車

pollute 污染

pond 池塘

pump 泵

R

race 比賽

rear light 車尾燈

（普：車後燈）

red 紅色

ride 騎

right 對 / 右

road signs 道路標誌

S

saddle 車座

signpost 指示牌

sister 姐姐 / 妹妹

slowly 慢慢地

sports car 跑車

square 廣場

stop 停

street 街道

suggests 提議

swans 天鵝

sweaty 滿身是汗

T

taxi 的士

tired 疲倦

traffic lights 交通燈

traffic officer 交通警察

train 火車

tries 嘗試

turn left 向左轉

turn right 向右轉

tyres 輪胎

V

vehicles 車輛

W

wait 等候

walk 走

watch out 小心

wheel 車輪

wrong 錯

Y

yellow 黃色

Z

zebra crossing 斑馬線

BYE-BYE, DEAR FRIENDS!
Goodbye, friends!
See you again!
看在一千塊莫澤雷勒乳酪的份上，你學得開心嗎？很開心，對不對？好極了！跟你一起跳舞唱歌我也很開心！我等着你下次繼續跟班哲文和潘朵拉一起玩一起學英語呀。現在要說再見了，當然是用英語說啦！

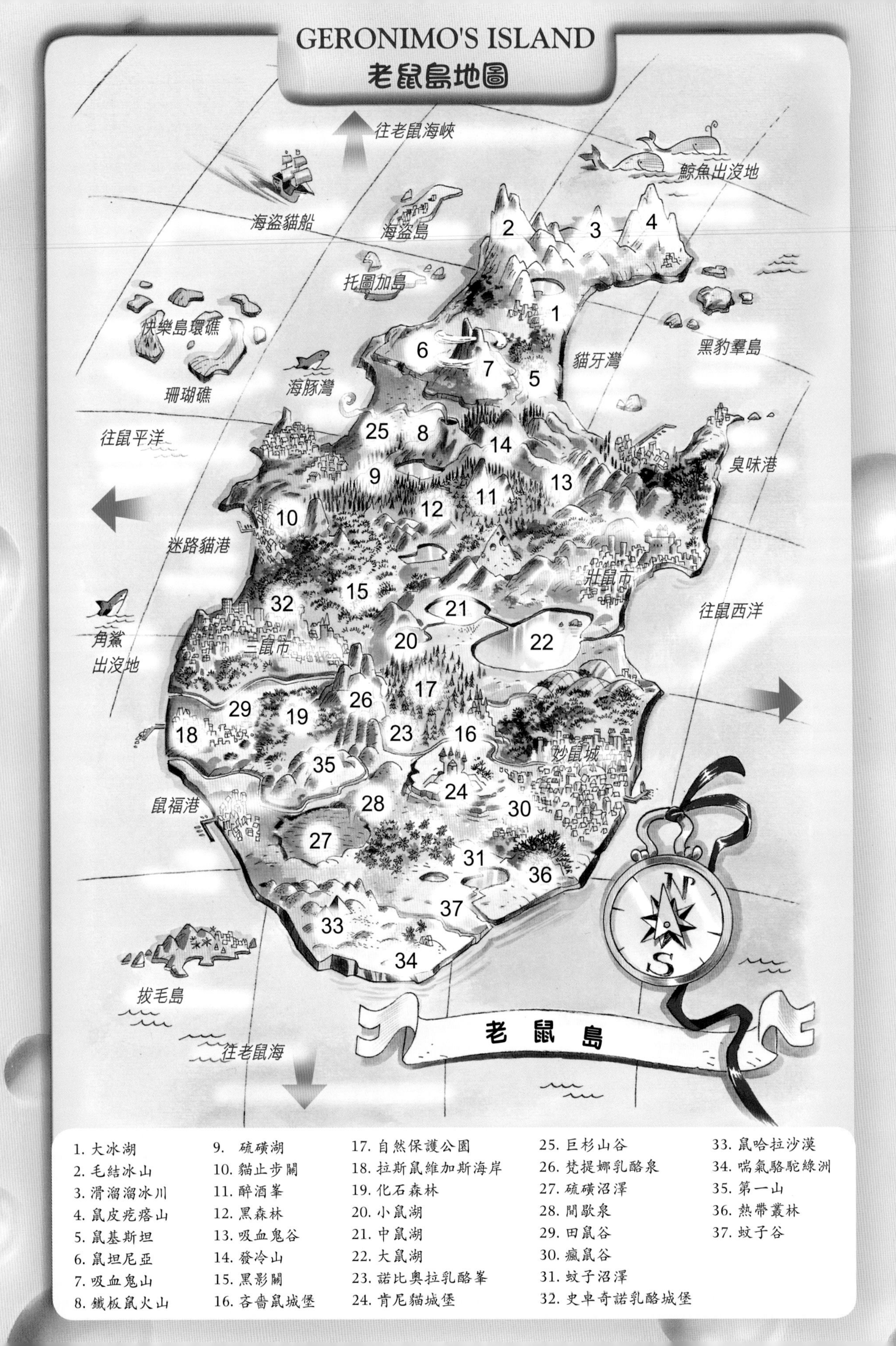

GERONIMO'S ISLAND
老鼠島地圖
往老鼠海峽
鯨魚出沒地
海盜貓船
海盜島
托圖加島
快樂島環礁
黑豹羣島
貓牙灣
海豚灣
珊瑚礁
往鼠平洋
臭味港
迷路貓港
壯鼠市
往鼠西洋
角鯊出沒地
三鼠市
妙鼠城
鼠福港
拔毛島
往老鼠海
老鼠島
1. 大冰湖
2. 毛結冰山
3. 滑溜溜冰川
4. 鼠皮疙瘩山
5. 鼠基斯坦
6. 鼠坦尼亞
7. 吸血鬼山
8. 鐵板鼠火山
9. 硫磺湖
10. 貓止步關
11. 醉酒峯
12. 黑森林
13. 吸血鬼谷
14. 發冷山
15. 黑影關
16. 吝嗇鼠城堡
17. 自然保護公園
18. 拉斯鼠維加斯海岸
19. 化石森林
20. 小鼠湖
21. 中鼠湖
22. 大鼠湖
23. 諾比奧拉乳酪峯
24. 肯尼貓城堡
25. 巨杉山谷
26. 梵提娜乳酪泉
27. 硫磺沼澤
28. 間歇泉
29. 田鼠谷
30. 瘋鼠谷
31. 蚊子沼澤
32. 史卓奇諾乳酪城堡
33. 鼠哈拉沙漠
34. 喘氣駱駝綠洲
35. 第一山
36. 熱帶叢林
37. 蚊子谷

Geronimo Stilton

EXERCISE BOOK

練習冊

想知道自己對 MOVING AROUND 掌握了多少，
趕快打開後面的練習完成它吧！

ENGLISH!

27 MOVING AROUND 我喜歡到處去

THE STREET
街道

✪ 看看下面的圖畫，選出代表答案的英文字母填在空格內，然後給圖畫填上顏色。

A. street　B. pavement　C. pedestrian
D. zebra crossing　E. traffic lights

CROSS THE ROAD
過馬路

✪ 行人過馬路時要注意些什麼？選出適當的字詞填在橫線上，完成句子。

left	right	walk	cross

1. Let's ________ on the pavement!

2. Let's ________ at the traffic lights!

3. Let's first look ________ and then ________ !

THE TRAFFIC LIGHTS
交通燈

✪ 1. 根據顏色詞，把交通燈填上相應的顏色，然後把交通燈和它代表的意思用線連起來。

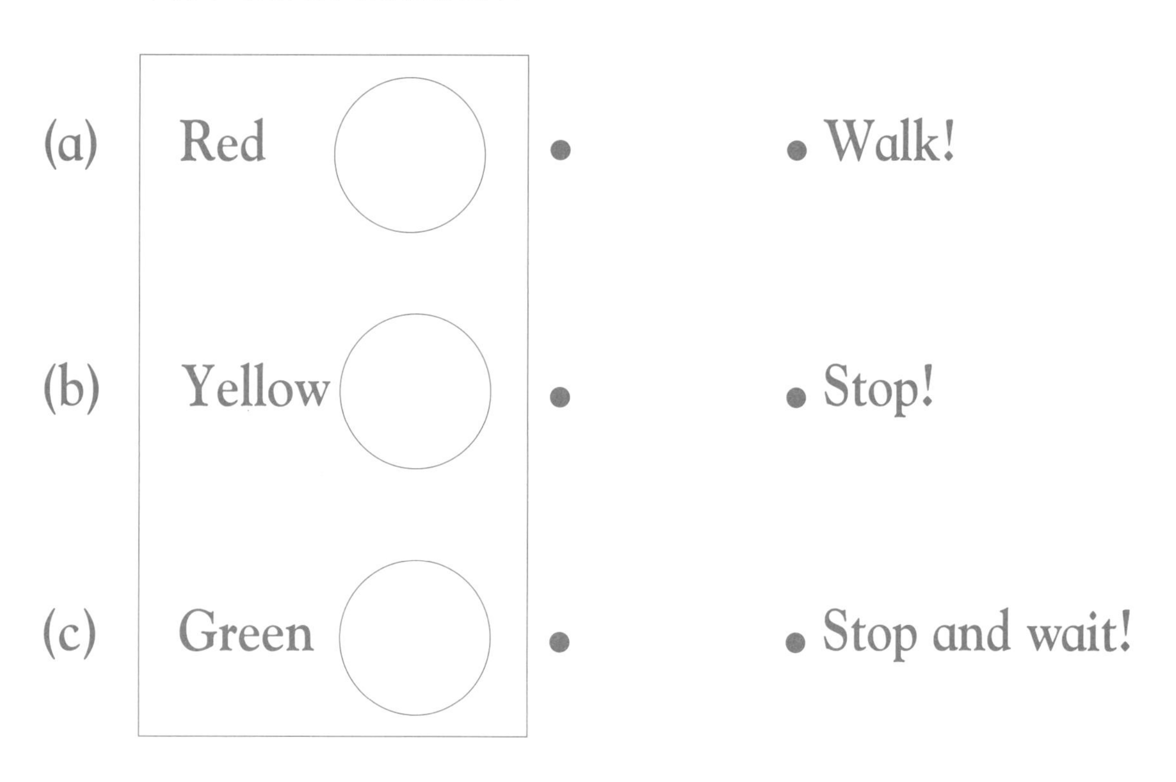

✪ 2. 判斷下面的句子是否正確。正確的，在空格內加✓；不正確的，在空格內加✗。

(a) Walk when the traffic lights are yellow. ☐

(b) Walk when the traffic lights are green. ☐

(c) Stop when the traffic lights are red. ☐

VEHICLES 車輛

✪ 你知道下面各種車輛的英文名稱嗎？選出適當的字詞填在橫線上。

car	motorcycle	ambulance	taxi
police car	fire engine	bus	train

1. 

____

2. 

____

3. 

____

4. 

____

5. 

____

6. 

____

7. 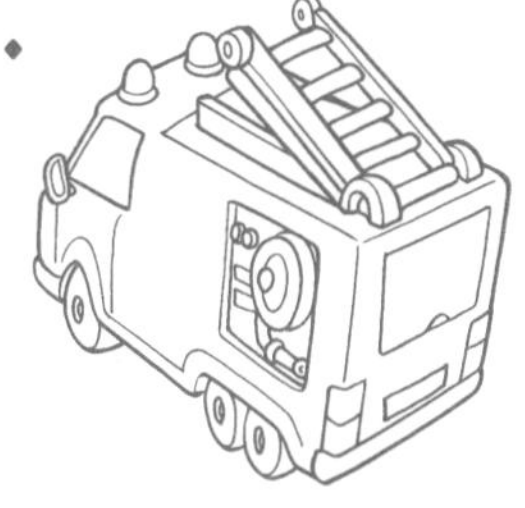

____

8. 

____

ROAD SIGNS 道路標誌

✪ 下面的道路標誌各代表什麼意思？把代表答案的英文字母填在空格內。

A. No parking.
B. Pedestrian area, no vehicles.
C. Children's crossing: slow down.
D. Parking.
E. Cycle lane for cyclists.
F. Stop!

MY BICYCLE 我的單車

✪ 看看下面的單車，你知道單車各部分的英文名稱嗎？把代表答案的英文字母填在空格內。

A. wheel	B. saddle	C. chain
D. brake	E. pedal	F. handlebars
G. rear light	H. tyre	

I CAN DRIVE 我會開車

✪ 根據圖畫，從下面選出適當的字詞填在橫線上。

car　　motorcycle　　her　　his

1. *I can drive a ______________ .*

2. Tea is driving __________ car.

3. *I can ride a ______________ .*

4. Ficcanaso is riding __________ motorcycle.

ANSWERS 答案

TEST 小測驗

1. (a) street (b) pavement (c) pedestrian (d) zebra crossing (e) traffic lights

2. (a) 我們在行人道上走吧！
   (b) 我們在交通燈那兒過馬路吧！
   (c) 橫過街道之前，要先看看右邊，再看看左邊。

3. (a) Stop! (b) Stop and wait! / Watch out! (c) Walk! / Go!

4. (a) bus (b) ambulance (c) fire engine (d) car (e) motorcycle / motorbike

5. A

6. (a) I can drive. (b) I can't drive.

EXERCISE BOOK 練習冊

P.1

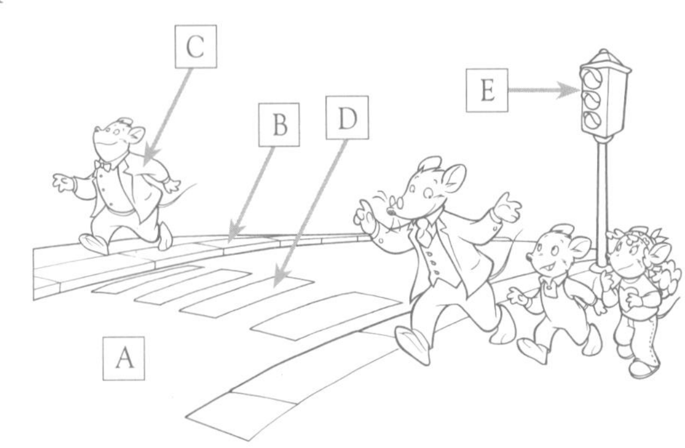

P.2

1. walk 2. cross 3. right, left

P.3

1. 填色：略
   (a) Stop! (b) Stop and wait!
   (c) Walk!

2. (a) ✗ (b) ✓ (c) ✓

P.4

1. police car 2. ambulance 3. taxi
4. motorcycle 5. car 6. bus
7. fire engine 8. train

P.5

1. B 2. E 3. C 4. A
5. F 6. D

P.7

1. car 2. her 3. motorcycle
4. his

P.6

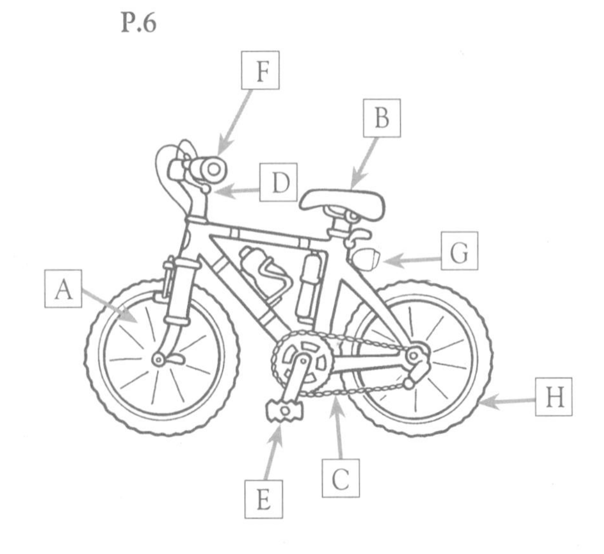